The Time Machine Girls
ERNESTINE TITO JONES

Jones, Ernestine Tito
The Time Machine Girls
Book Two: Never Give Up;
Also published as Follow Failure
Website: www.ernestinetitojones.com

The Time Machine Girls

2

Never Give Up

Chapter One

Ugh! The tips of Hazel's fingers were caught again. "I'll never get this right," she said, yanking her pinkie and ring finger free from the tangle of threads in front of her. "I can't believe I have to pull everything apart and start all over again." She threw her friendship bracelet across the room, crossed her arms, and flopped down on the couch. "That's it. I give up," she said.

Even though she was pretty sure she was tying her strings exactly the way the book said to do it, she couldn't get her knots right. So instead of a friendship bracelet, she just had a failure.

Bess shrugged. "I'm having no problems," she said, sitting on the floor in front of the coffee table. She was wearing a striped superhero dress. Her hair was up in what Bess was calling her "superhero ponytail," but Hazel barely saw a regular ponytail. Hardly any hair was in the hair tie part.

Hazel looked over at the wadded glob of random twists and knots her sister that was supposed to be a friendship bracelet and rolled her eyes.

How on earth were they even related? Bess was a six-year-old mess. She never even tried to think things through or get things right. She just did whatever she wanted. Hazel knew there were rules to making a friendship bracelet, and her sister should at least try to follow them.

Bess held up her tangled messy bracelet and inspected it from all angles. One side was thicker than the other and somehow there were strands hanging down in weird spots like hair. "Perfect," she said, grinning proudly at her masterpiece.

"Bess, you don't even have a pattern going," Hazel replied, picking up the bracelet-making book from off the couch and bringing it over to where her sister was sitting on the floor.

"See?" Hazel said slowly so her sister would understand, running her finger along a page that had a beautiful turquoise-and-black bracelet on it. "It's supposed to look something like this. You're just pulling and tying random colors together. And you're not even knotting them right. You need to start all over again."

"Nope," Bess replied. "This is exactly how I like it. I'm making it for you because I love you so much."

Hazel forced a smile. "Th-th-thanks," she said, unsure of how to tell her sister there was no way she was wearing that lumpy piece of weirdness.

Bess motioned toward Froggenstein who was sitting comfortably in the small plastic aquarium their mother had given Bess to keep her pet frog in. He had a clumped-up ball of yellow, orange, and pink thread sitting in front of him with a green bead tied loosely in the middle of it. "I already made a bracelet for Froggenstein, and now I'm making one for you. I'm going to add a special bead to all of them. Froggenstein's bead is green. Yours will be orange... It's for our club. We're going to be the Time Machine Girls," she said proudly, adjusting her thick glasses, "and Time Machine frog."

Hazel shook her head. "Bess, we agreed we're not going in the attic anymore. Remember?"

Ever since they'd gotten back from their first time machine trip the day before yesterday, the girls agreed not to go in the attic or use the time machine again. It was against the rules to go in the attic. It was probably dangerous to use the time machine, and Hazel knew something Bess didn't. Somewhere in their grandparents' old farmhouse was a family secret their parents didn't want them to find out about.

As the older sister, Hazel knew it was her job to make sure they didn't accidentally find it, whatever it was. And Hazel had an idea it had something to do with the attic, the time machine, and the trunk Bess found that was full of old stuff their grandfather probably stole from history.

"Come on...." Bess begged, adding more tangles into the bracelet she was making. "Let's just see if the trunk is open."

Hazel shook her head. "We already checked the trunk when we got back, and it was locked."

"Please...." Bess whined, friendship bracelet string somehow dangling from her messy blonde ponytail.

Hazel crossed her arms. "No, Bess. It's locked for a reason. So forget about the attic and the trunk already. We're not going in the time machine again and that's final!" She yelled.

"*The what machine?*"

The girls looked up. They hadn't realized their mother and grandparents were standing behind them.

Their mother had been carrying empty boxes, but she fumbled and dropped them to the floor as she spoke. "The w-w-what machine?" she repeated, picking them back up again. "What did you say?"

Their grandfather's eyes slanted into angry darts, and their grandmother's mouth hung open.

Hazel gasped. She should never have said that so loudly. How long had they been standing there? And what had they heard?

Chapter Two

Hazel laughed and smoothed out her perfectly combed bun, trying to think of something to say. "It-it's just a game we play," she said.

Hazel hated lying. She was the responsible, honest one in the family and honest people didn't do that. Still, she couldn't tell them the truth. She couldn't tell her mother that while she and Bess were snooping around in the attic, they'd found a time machine, and decided to take it for a ride. They weren't even supposed to be in the attic.

Hazel's mouth felt dry as she spoke. She coughed a little. "When we get bored here, we do a lot of pretending. You know... kid stuff like that." She put her hand on Bess's shoulder, hoping her sister would catch on. "Isn't that right, Bess?"

Bess was busy tying more knots into her friendship blob and barely looked up. "Yeah, we like to pretend there's a time machine in the attic and a trunk full of stolen stuff..."

Hazel elbowed her sister and gave her a dirty look. Why was Bess such a mixed-up mess? She always told the truth when she should be lying and told lies when she should be telling the truth, not that they ever should be lying.

Bess elbowed Hazel back. "You didn't let me finish. I was going to say a trunk full of stolen stuff that green monsters with big snotty noses took from me and Hazel." Bess laughed so hard she almost fell onto the coffee table.

"Hazel and me," their mother said, correcting Bess's English. As a teacher, she did that a lot. She sighed and kissed both girls on the head. "Th-thank goodness," she added under her breath. The color returned to her face and she no longer seemed like she might pass out. "You're both very imaginative."

She looked down at the empty boxes in her hands. "You're probably wondering what I'm doing with these boxes."

Hazel shook her head "yes," even though she wasn't wondering.

"Your grandparents and I are off to clean out the old shed. Would you girls like to help?"

Grandpa shook his head when their mother said that. His eyes looked like tiny little dots hidden under bushy caterpillars. "They can't come. It's too dangerous."

"Nonsense," their mother replied. "The old shed isn't dangerous at all, and it'll be good for them to help out. Besides, you heard them; they're bored. They'd probably love to take a break from their bracelets and look through all the old treasures we have stashed around here, like my old swimming trophies, that big box of photos we found, and the scrapbooks..."

"They can't come." Their grandfather repeated, his lips barely moved through his thick beard. He turned his head so he was facing the girls, staring them down.

Hazel shivered. Her grandfather always scared her. He was a big man who never smiled and barely spoke, and when he did say something, it always seemed angry. Why was he angry all the time? And why couldn't they go into the shed, not that looking at old swimming trophies seemed like fun to Hazel.

The wrinkles around her grandfather's eyes seemed to swirl all the way up to his forehead. "They can't come and that's that." It was almost as if he was warning them, and then... he winked.

He must've had something in his eye because there was no way that was a real wink. A wink that meant something.

Still, it was definitely a wink. And if Hazel hadn't known better she could have sworn her crazy old grandpa had smiled when he'd done it too. But who could tell with such a thick beard? She must have been imagining things. Why would their grumpy, mean grandpa wink and smile at them?

He grumbled something under his breath as he looked at Hazel. "Behind the glass shop..."

Hazel's hope faded. The wink hadn't meant anything after all. Their grandfather was just being as crazy as people said he was.

"Come on, Burt," their grandmother said, touching his arm and leading him out the door. His feet shuffled as he walked, and Hazel felt sorry for him. Poor crazy Grandpa.

Their mother followed, still complaining about how the shed wasn't dangerous at all and not understanding why her father had to be so stubborn.

Just before their grandmother closed the front door, she stuck her head back into the living room. "Have fun," she said. "There's homemade lemonade and biscuits if you get hungry. We'll be right in the shed if you need us."

Hazel smiled and forced herself to say

"thank you" to her grandmother, even though she wasn't the least bit interested in the biscuits and lemonade. Just the word "homemade" made her remember those sour pickles she ate the other day. Her face puckered thinking about them.

As soon as the door closed, Bess jumped up. "You saw that wink Grandpa gave us. He knows that we know about the time machine, and he wants us to go back into the attic."

What? Now she knew her sister was crazy too. Even if their grandfather had winked on purpose, it hadn't meant what Bess thought it meant. Hazel was sure of it.

Bess dropped her friendship bracelet and headed for the stairs.

"Oh no!" Hazel gasped, running after

her. Maybe it was time she told Bess the real reason they couldn't go back into the attic. Maybe it was time Bess knew about the secret.

Chapter Three

Hazel ran ahead of Bess and stopped her at the staircase. She stretched her hands out so that one reached the wall while the other held onto the banister. "Bess, there's something I should tell you."

Bess smirked. "I already know what it is. You're going to tell on me again."

Hazel scrunched her face up when

her sister said that. Sure, she hadn't been the nicest to Bess since they got to the farmhouse. But then, Bess never followed any rules, and Hazel had to watch her all the time while their mother helped their grandparents clean up their house so they could move.

"No," Hazel replied, taking a deep breath. "I said I'd throw out my tattletale notebook, and I meant it, but you also agreed you wouldn't break the rules on purpose anymore."

Bess looked down at her feet. "It's boring here. The time machine is the one fun thing we have."

"I know, but there's a reason we shouldn't use it anymore. I probably should've told you this sooner, but there's a secret."

Bess looked up when Hazel said "secret" like she was finally interested in the conversation. She sat down on one of the stairs. "Go on. What's the secret?"

Hazel sat next to her. The old wooden staircase of their grandparents' farmhouse creaked under their weight. "I heard Mom and Dad talking before we left for the summer," Hazel began, not sure how to tell her sister. "M-m-mom didn't want us to come with her to the farmhouse."

"What? That's silly. Why?"

Hazel ran her fingers through Bess's hair, which probably hadn't been brushed all day even though their mother told her to brush it. Hazel hit tangle after tangle.

"Mom said there was an awful family

secret she didn't want us to find. It was something about Grandpa, something she couldn't relive. I'm pretty sure it has something to do with the attic and the time machine."

Bess sat there, listening. Hazel looked at her bright white tennis shoes. She couldn't look at Bess. She knew she was disappointing her sister.

"So you see?" Hazel finally said, getting up. "That's the reason we can't go in the attic anymore. There's something in there that'll hurt Mom. Or us. Come on. Let's go get something to eat."

Bess looked up toward the attic. "Wow," she said, standing up and walking toward the living room. "I don't want to hurt Mom."

The girls went into the living room. Bess picked up her friendship bracelet and stared at it sadly. "I guess we can't be the Time Machine Girls anymore. We were going to be like superheroes through time."

Hazel tried to cheer her up. "We can still pretend, and we can still have fun. I promise."

Bess grabbed another piece of thread and knotted it into her tangled messy bracelet. "You want to make more friendship bracelets?" she asked.

"No way," Hazel said, pulling a piece of string out of her sister's hair. "It's too hard for me. I'm giving up, but let's try one of Grandma's biscuits. Are you hungry?"

She went into the kitchen and pulled out two plates, placing a homemade biscuit

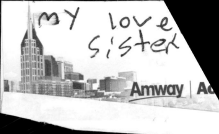

on each.

Maybe she had misjudged her little sister. Here she'd thought that telling Bess about the family secret would make her even more curious to uncover it. But instead, Bess had understood. Maybe that kid was finally growing up.

Hazel opened the cupboard and pulled out two cups for the lemonade.

BANG!!!!! THUD!!!!!!

Oh no! Not again. The sounds definitely came from the attic.

Bess hadn't learned anything after all. She had just been waiting for Hazel to turn her back. Hazel knew she was about to follow her sister into the attic, again.

Chapter Four

Hazel ran up the stairs to the second floor then up the narrow dark stairwell that led to the attic. She stopped just before she entered and listened for a second by the door.

"Funny," she thought, catching her breath. "Why don't I hear anything?" Still, she knew Bess was in there somewhere.

Slowly, she opened the door and peeked inside.

"Beatrice Samantha Smith, you need to get out of the attic right now," she said, flicking on the light switch. "Or I will tell Mom, and I mean it."

She wondered if she really did mean it.

The attic looked the same as it had a couple of days ago when the girls were up there last. Old mechanical parts and boxes were stacked along the walls, and a bookcase sat off in a dark corner still full of Grandpa's weird books about time traveling.

Hazel slowly walked over to the bookcase, her shoes creaking over the floor, and quickly looked through the books before Bess popped out of her hiding spot and saw her. Last week when she and Bess were in the attic, Hazel had noticed a book with a mysterious paper sticking out of it like a bookmark. She had wanted to look at it then, but she didn't have time. Maybe, she had time now.

Hazel shook her head as she read over the titles of the books again:

The Art of Time Travel

How to Make a Time Machine in Six Easy Steps

It all seemed so crazy and she still couldn't believe the time machine had actually worked, but it had. And ever since that day when she and Bess traveled back in time to meet George Washington, her mind had raced with questions. But the biggest question she had was *why*? Why was there a time machine in their grandparents' attic? Why had there been a trunk full of stolen stuff from history? It was all so confusing.

She found the book with the bookmark, and read the title out loud. "*The Hidden Dangers in Time Traveling.*"

She looked around to make sure Bess wasn't watching her then quickly reached for the book. She had to work fast. This might be part of the secret. Hazel had to stand on her tiptoes to get to the shelf with the book on it, but even then she could barely reach it. She finally grabbed the book along with a handful of dust, and what felt like a cobweb. Gross...

She dropped the book and held in her

scream, wiping her hands of on her jeans.
She searched through her pocket for the
hand sanitizer, hitting the edge of the
bookcase and knocking over three more
books. *Bang! Crash! Thud!*

Dust floated through the air like tiny
bugs. Hazel coughed on dust, trying not to
think about how many germs she'd just
swallowed.

The books landed right in front of the
old trunk, its lid still closed and latched like
before. Bess had said she saw a bunch of
stuff in there: swords, helmets, gadgets,
George Washington's cherry-tree ax... And
even though her sister lied a lot, Hazel
believed her when she said she saw all
those things in this trunk, especially when
the trunk had suddenly become

mysteriously locked. Obviously, somebody didn't want them snooping around the time machine anymore. All the more reason to leave things alone.

Still, she couldn't help but wonder if it was still locked.

"Just one quick pull to see if it'll open, and then I'll stop trying," she told herself, putting her hand on the top of it to gain her balance as she looked it over. The faded green trunk was covered in dust and spider webs too.

Hazel yanked her hand back and wiped it on the sides of her jeans. Taking out a small bottle of hand sanitizer from her pocket, she squirted a large dab into her palm.

"Disgusting," she said to herself,

waving her hands around to dry them. The hand sanitizer smelled like lemon, which was a lot better than the smell of the old attic.

Shadows bounced off the walls and seemed to follow her every move. Hazel knew she shouldn't be in there.

Slowly and quietly, she unhooked the two latches on the side of the trunk, knowing every second of the way that she shouldn't be doing it. This was definitely against the rules. Nervous sweat dripped down her forehead as she held her breath...

"Boo!" A voice from behind her said, causing Hazel to lose her balance and fall over onto the trunk. She immediately got up and turned around. It was Bess.

"Bess!" she said, standing up. Her

shirt was covered in dust. "Now I have germs all over me thanks to you. Gross! Where were you?"

Rrrrrrrrrr-ibbbbet!

"I just went to our room to get a cricket for Froggenstein's lunch. You asked if we were getting hungry, and Froggenstein was. But now, if Mom asks, I followed *you* into the attic." Bess laughed.

Hazel rolled her eyes, but it was technically true. No sense in tattling now.

Bess bunched her face up. "Why are you in the attic anyway? I thought you just got done telling me about a family secret in here that we're not supposed to find out about."

Hazel kicked the book behind her so Bess wouldn't see it. "I thought I was following *you* in here. It sounded like you knocked something over or broke something in here."

Bess shook her head. "Nope. Why do you always think I'm breaking the rules?"

"Because you usually are! And I heard a crash."

"Oh that," Bess said. "I had to stand on a chair to reach the special beads on my dresser, and I jumped down when I found them. It was louder than I thought." She handed Hazel her friendship bracelet lump. It was yellow, orange, and purple with an orange bead tied to the middle of it. "Ta-da! It's perfect now. Here you go."

"Th-th-thanks." Hazel said, embarrassed that she'd misjudged her sister and was the real reason they were standing in the attic right now.

"So was the trunk locked?" Bess asked.

"I don't know. I didn't check," Hazel replied.

"But, you were about to," Bess said, smiling.

Hazel headed for the door. She'd have to look at the book and the paper later. "You're right. I broke the rules this time, and I'm sorry. It wasn't okay to do that. We should leave."

Hazel turned around and looked back at her little sister. Bess was sitting in front of their grandfather's old army trunk. And it was open.

Chapter Five

"Whoa," Bess said, staring at the open trunk. "I told you Grandpa's wink meant something! The trunk is unlocked."

The trunk was unlocked, all right. But it was empty.

Hazel walked back over to Bess and sat down. "I think Grandpa's wink meant he knew we'd been up here and he's stopping us from going in the time machine again by emptying the trunk."

Bess turned her head to the side, confused. "Why wouldn't he just leave the trunk locked? That stopped us too."

Hazel hadn't thought of that. "I don't know. Maybe he wants us to know that he knows what we've been up to..."

Their grandfather's wink hadn't meant *go ahead and use the time machine again*. It was a cruel wink, the kind of wink Hazel should have expected from their grumpy grandfather. That wink said, "I know you used the time machine, and I've stopped you from ever using it again."

It was for the best anyway. It was hard enough to watch her little sister here at the farmhouse. She couldn't imagine all the danger they'd be running into if they were traveling through time. As far as Hazel was concerned, the girls were lucky to have made it back in one piece and in time for dinner the last time they went out.

Hazel put her hand on her sister's shoulder. "Well, that was fun while it lasted. Not too many people can say they've traveled through time to meet George Washington, even though we can't say that to anyone, ever. Still, we should be thankful we have that memory."

She looked over at her sister, fully expecting to see Bess's thick glasses fogging up with tears of failure. Instead, her sister was back on her feet, leaning over the trunk.

"What are you doing?" Hazel asked.

"It's empty. Let's go."

"You can give up if you want to," Bess replied, feeling her hand along the black metal bottom of the trunk. "But not me. Looking for a secret is a lot more fun than making bracelets."

Hazel rolled her eyes. She should never have told Bess about the family secret. It had just made her crazy with curiosity.

And she was acting crazy all right. Hazel watched her sister run her hands along the sides and bottom of the empty trunk. What was she doing – looking for a trap door?

Hazel picked up the mysterious book while her sister was busy acting crazy. Quietly, she took it over by the attic window and sat down next to a box of old machine parts. The light streamed in just enough for her to see, but hopefully not enough for Bess to notice her. She doubted that the bookmark had anything to do with the secret anyway, and she didn't want to have to explain things to her sister.

She flipped the book open to the page it was marking, noticing that the bookmark wasn't a note after all, and it wasn't a bookmark. It was half of a ripped-up old flyer of some sort, an advertisement for a county fair.

Come see the world's first time machine at the fair this Saturday! Local professor will be holding a public demonstration of what he says is the world's first working time machine...

Hazel had no idea what that could have meant. Who was this local professor? She thought her grandfather had built this time machine, and he wasn't a professor; he was a farmer. Her grandfather must've stolen the time machine too – along with everything that used to be in the trunk! Could that be the big family secret?

Hazel looked up. Her sister was grinning and holding a small group of thin black wires.

"The trunk wasn't empty after all," she said. "Grandpa left us these."

Hazel quickly closed the book and stuffed the paper into her pocket before Bess could ask her about it, instantly wishing she'd have thought to see what page it had been on. But it was too late now. She casually went over to the bookshelf and put the book back.

Bess was too busy staring at the strings she was holding to care what Hazel had been doing.

Strings?

Poor Bess. Hazel didn't have the heart to tell her those were probably just friendship bracelet threads that had fallen out of her messy hair and into the empty trunk.

"Let me see those," Hazel said, taking one of the pieces of thread from her sister's hand. She ran her fingers along it. It was the most interesting thread she'd ever seen. It was coated in a black, somewhat sticky substance that rubbed off a little under the warmth of her fingers, and it seemed very fragile. Maybe these were more than random. But what were they? One thing was for sure, they definitely didn't come from a friendship bracelet.

Chapter Six

"See? It pays to keep looking!" Bess said, holding up one of the threads and examining it from every angle. "These sure are strange."

Hazel knew that just because a thread was strange didn't mean it was going to start the time machine. Besides, they shouldn't be trying to start the time machine anyway, especially since she just saw there was a whole book on the hidden dangers of it. Now, she wished more than ever that she'd noticed the page the bookmark had been on.

"I guess it's possible Grandpa just missed those when he cleaned out the trunk," Hazel said. "But I'm not sure they're enough to start the time machine."

Bess smiled. "There's only one way to find out." Bess carefully cupped the fragile black strings in her hands and marched them over to the time machine that stood off in the corner, humming what she probably thought was a superhero song.

Hazel giggled at her sister, but followed her. Even though every part of her knew she should be stopping Bess instead of helping her, Hazel found herself lifting the machine's dome lid and opening the secret compartment under the control panel so her sister could put the strings in there. She was having fun, which was something neither of them had enough of at the farmhouse.

A couple of days ago, they figured out that if they put one of the stolen pieces of history in the secret compartment, the time machine would go right to the day the piece was stolen. Or, at least, that's how it had seemed to work.

"We'll just play in the time machine for a few minutes, then we'll leave. We won't really go anywhere," Hazel said. She doubted the time machine would even start up with the strings.

Bess didn't answer. She was still humming.

"Did you hear me, Bess," she said when Bess finished closing up the secret compartment. "We're just going to check to see if these strings start the machine up, and nothing else. We're not actually going anywhere, even if it does start up."

Bess grabbed Froggenstein and bounced into the old wheelchair that was the seat for the time machine. "Ready?" Bess asked, giving a big thumbs-up. "We're just going to see if the strings start the time machine, but nothing else." Then she hit the green button.

Slowly, the engine started rumbling under Hazel's feet. First, short bursts of power that grew until the whole house was shaking violently from the force of the machine. Hazel was surprised to find herself smiling.

It was working! She hugged her sister.

"I can't believe it, Bess." Hazel yelled over the rumbling of the time machine. "You were right!"

Bess scooted over so Hazel could sit down. "Good thing Grandpa has bad eyes and missed those strings!" she yelled.

Hazel sat down, wondering if it really was a good thing their grandpa had bad eyes. She looked for a button to turn the machine off. "We need to find the off button," she yelled over the sound of the machine.

Bess strapped them both in and

began pushing buttons.

Hazel put her hands over the controls to stop her sister, but she might have hit a button.

A bright light flashed. Blip. They were gone.

Chapter Seven

Hazel blinked. A cool wind blew by her face and a branch scratched at her arm. Where was she? She looked up. Bess was smiling at her.

"It worked!" Bess said. "I'm so glad you decided to use the time machine again."

Hazel couldn't believe her ears. *What*

had her sister just said? Was she crazy?

"Bess, I don't know what you're talking about. I told you we were just going to see if the strings started the time machine again but nothing else. We weren't supposed to go anywhere."

"Then why did you get in and hit a button," Bess asked, adjusting her glasses. Her big brown eyes seemed genuinely surprised and confused.

"You hit the button," Hazel said.

"I was trying to turn it off," Bess said. "And, I followed *you* into the attic, remember? I should start a tattletale notebook."

Hazel ignored her sister. Bess had a point, though, whether she liked it or not. But it didn't matter whose idea it was anymore, anyway. They were here, wherever here was. And they needed to return the strings and get back.

"Where do you think we are?" Bess asked, yanking a twig from her messy blonde hair and throwing it down on the grass underneath them.

"I have no idea," Hazel replied.

Once again, the time machine had landed in a clump of bushes. The domed hatch had popped open and branches and leaves were everywhere, scratching at the girls. Hazel pulled them away from her face and looked around.

They were sitting in the middle of a large fenced-in yard, staring up at a long, rectangular white house that had smaller buildings on the sides of it.

Loud voices came from the main house.

"Come on," Bess said, unlatching her seatbelt and getting out. "Let's see what's going on!" She pushed her way out of the bushes, and began skipping toward the house.

Rrrrrrr-ibbet

"You're forgetting Froggenstein!" Hazel yelled after her sister. For someone who loved her frog so much, she sure forgot him a lot. Hazel picked up the small plastic aquarium then thought better about it. Froggenstein had water and shade where he was in the time machine. They should probably just leave him there.

Leaving Froggenstein, Hazel carefully grabbed the black wires from the hidden compartment and ran to catch up to her sister. Whatever these thin black wires were, their grandfather had stolen them and they needed to be returned, even though Hazel wasn't nearly as enthusiastic about the whole adventure as Bess was.

"Wait for me!" Hazel yelled as she ran.

The air was cool and crisp, and the leaves on the surrounding trees were changing color into their red, yellow, and brown autumn hues. If Hazel had to guess, she would say it was sometime in the fall, but what year? And whose weird white house was this?

Bess had already reached the front porch when Hazel caught up to her. Loud conversation could be heard from inside, and even though Hazel couldn't make out anything that was being said, it sounded like someone was angry about something.

Bess didn't seem to notice. She was busy twirling around one of the thick white columns on the front porch.

"These are fun," she said loudly.

"Shhhh." Hazel quickly hushed her sister. "We've never talked about this, but we need to have a plan. We can't just barge into this house and say 'Hello, everyone. We're from the future. We need to return these strings.' They will think we're crazy. Maybe we should peek in a window or something."

"You're right," Bess replied. Hazel couldn't believe it. Did her sister just say she was right about something?

The girls pressed their faces against one of the large rectangular windows on the porch. Hazel couldn't make out much, but she thought she saw several long tables with machinery and wires on them. Men rushed from one table to the next.

"What in the world are they doing?" Bess asked.

"I don't know," Hazel whispered. "But if we meet them, just remember we can't mention anything about the time machine or coming from the future, okay?"

"Okay," Bess said, nodding in agreement. "But what do we say instead?"

Hazel hadn't thought of that one, and this was not the time to be thinking about it. The voices from the inside seemed to be getting louder and closer. Hazel motioned for her sister to follow her off the porch.

Although the girls tried to be quick, they weren't quick enough. The door to the large house swung open just as a booming voice said, "There are no rules here. We're trying to accomplish something!"

Three men stepped onto the porch, laughing. Their faces dropped when they saw the girls.

"Run and hide!" Bess yelled, jumping off the porch and taking off around the side of the house. Hazel had never seen her little sister run so fast.

Hazel wanted to run too, but for some reason, she couldn't get her feet to move. She stood frozen in front of the men.

Hazel swallowed hard and tried to put on a brave smile. "H-h-hello," she stammered.

The three men were all in heavy, dark suits with jackets, and were about her father's age. One had a beard, one had a thick mustache, and the one in the middle was clean shaven. None of them looked happy.

"What do we have here?" the bearded men said, grabbing the black wires from Hazel's hand. "These kids are either thieves or spies!"

Thieves or Spies?!

Somehow, Hazel knew they were in big trouble this time.

Chapter Eight

Hazel felt her eyes fill with tears. She wasn't a thief or a spy. In fact, she always followed the rules.

The man examined the wires. "These are ours all right," he said to the other men. They nodded in agreement. He turned back to Hazel. "Young lady, do you mind telling us how you got these filaments?"

"Fill a whats?" Hazel replied. "I don't know what that is."

"That's hard to believe," the man without a beard or mustache said. He looked at Hazel as if she were a thief. "Are you from one of the newspapers?"

Hazel shook her head. "No. Honest. My sister and I were just playing and we found them. We thought they probably came from your house."

The bearded man laughed. Hazel wondered if they had all been joking about the "thief and spy" part. She didn't think it was funny.

He went on. "House? This is no house! This is an invention factory! The largest of its kind. So, you're telling me you have no idea where you're at?"

"No," Hazel replied.

"And you have no idea who this great man is in front of you?" The man pointed to his friend in the middle the one with no beard or mustache. He had short dark hair, a long-sleeved white shirt, and a bow tie. Hazel guessed the man was someone famous, but she had no clue who he was.

"No, I'm sorry," Hazel said, shaking her head while she looked at the man. "Who are you? And where are we?"

Suddenly Bess popped her head from around the side of the building. "We'd also like to know what year it is too, please, because we're from the future," she said then ducked her head back behind the building so no one on the porch could see her anymore.

All three men laughed.

Hazel rolled her eyes. "Bess, I think you can come up here now. We're not in trouble..." Hazel looked at the three men again, still not sure if they were joking. "I mean, I hope we're not in trouble. Are we?" she asked.

The famous man smiled. "No. You're not in any trouble. This is a glorious day and nothing can mess it up for us now. You've come at the perfect time. You're about to witness history."

Hazel smiled. The man had no idea just how right he was.

Suddenly Bess's head appeared again, then the rest of her. She hurried up the stairs and over to her sister. ""Glor-ous, huh? What does that mean? What happened today?"

The younger man with the mustache motioned around the porch. "You're standing at Menlo Park, Thomas Edison's famous laboratory. It's 1879, and this man here is, of course, Thomas Edison. You've probably heard of him... the Wizard of Menlo Park?"

Hazel took a step back, amazed once again that the time machine had worked. She couldn't believe it was actually 1879 and she was standing on a porch with Thomas Edison.

"So, you're a wizard?" Bess asked. "Show us some magic."

"Bess, stop," Hazel said, elbowing her sister. "That's rude, and he's not a real wizard."

"Oh, so he's pretending, like me. I'm a superhero today," she said, holding out her hand for Thomas Edison to shake. "A Time Machine Girl, only that part's not pretend."

Hazel shook her head as Thomas Edison shook Bess's hand. Thankfully, it didn't look like any of the men believed her about the time machine.

Hazel knew a little bit about the famous man in the middle. She'd done a report on him last year in her history class. He had invented the light bulb, but he didn't look a thing like the picture she'd printed out for her report. This man was young. The picture she'd used was of an old, balding, grumpy man, like her grandpa but without the beard.

Thomas Edison rolled up his sleeves. "Today is an important day at Menlo Park," he said. "We've been working on the incandescent lamp for some time now, and I think that after 1,000 failed attempts, we've finally figured it out today."

Hazel couldn't believe it. *Thomas Edison had failed more than 1,000 times at something, and he still kept trying to get it right...*

"The what lamp?" Bess asked, scrunching her face. "Sorry to tell you all this, but whatever you're talking about isn't going to be important in the future." Bess pointed toward the time machine. "And we should know. That's where we just came from. The future."

"What are you talking about," one of

the men asked.

"I've been trying to tell you. We came in a time machine."

The three men's mouths dropped open. They looked shocked like they might be believing her now.

Hazel shushed her sister. *Why did Bess always have to have such a big mouth?*

Chapter Nine

An autumn breeze blew onto the porch, sending the scent of leaves and dirt circling through the air. It was a cool day, but Hazel's face was red and hot, which happened a lot when she was nervous. She looked up at the men. They were still staring at her for an explanation.

She laughed. "My sister has the

craziest imagination. The future? Six-year-olds are so silly." Hazel shook her head, still laughing. She slapped her hand on her knee to show just how funny that was.

The men looked confused and curious until Mr. Edison began laughing along with Hazel. The other two men laughed too.

"We could use more humor around here," Mr. Edison said. He pointed to his friends. "These men are Charles and Francis, two of my assistants."

Hazel shook the men's hands, "Nice to meet you. I'm Hazel and this is Bess."

"Where are you all from?" Francis, the younger assistant with the mustache asked. He looked right at Bess's superhero dress when he asked it.

Hazel hadn't thought of what to say when asked that question. If she told them they lived around here, they would probably know she was lying. This is a small village, and they probably knew everyone here. She didn't know what to say...

Bess put her hands on her hips, "I already told you. The future."

The three men laughed again.

"That's right. We'd forgotten," Mr. Edison said, winking at the other men. He motioned around the large fenced-in area that surrounded the house. "Go ahead and give these ladies a tour, Francis," Mr. Edison said. "Show them the whole operation. We'll see if we can't impress that little one with something we have here in the past."

Bess shrugged. "I guess you can try."

Hazel elbowed her. "Please be quiet and polite," she said under her breath.

"I'm already both!" Bess yelled back.

Mr. Edison and Charles walked back into the house, leaving the girls standing on the porch with Francis.

There were several other houses and shacks on the property. And Hazel was thrilled to hear they were going to get to peek around at all of them.

"Just don't touch anything," Francis said, looking directly at Bess. Hazel laughed to herself. How did he already know her sister so well?

Francis went on, "This place is full of breakable and expensive things, and we don't normally let kids run around the laboratory, so you can look, but you can't touch. Like Mr. Edison said this is a very important day at Menlo Park, and in a minute, you'll see why."

Hazel was really going to have to watch Bess on this one. She couldn't let her sister mess history up, especially not one of Thomas Edison's experiments on whatever important day today was.

"That's funny," Francis said as they followed him off the porch and around the side of the house. "You're the second unexpected guest we've had today. Maybe you know the first one. He was a man with a beard. Thought he said his name was Burt."

That was their grandpa's name!

Could Francis be talking about him? But how? Hazel thought about it for a second. Even though their grandfather had taken those black wires years before she and Bess had found them, he originally took them from the same day she and Bess were at, right now. Were they about to see a younger Grandpa?

Hazel gave Bess a knowing look. Was she thinking what Hazel was thinking?

"Sorry. Don't know the guy," Bess said to Francis, shrugging.

Chapter Ten

Hazel wanted to tell her little sister that she thought the other stranger was probably their grandfather. She also wanted to ask Francis more questions about the stranger's visit, but she decided to wait until the right time. She wasn't exactly sure how to do it without making Francis very suspicious.

Francis pointed to a small shack around the back of the house. "This is the glassblower's shop," he said.

"The what?" Bess asked, pressing her face against the window of the small shack so she could see inside.

"The glassblower makes glass in whatever shape Mr. Edison tells him to make, and whenever he needs it," Francis replied. "Back there's the machine shop. When Mr. Edison draws up plans for an invention, he gives them to the machinist, and he makes whatever Mr. Edison wants right here on the property."

"Wow," Hazel said, thinking back on her report. She wrote about Thomas Edison's inventions, but she never knew this much went into them. "I had no idea so many people worked with Mr. Edison."

"Look around," Francis said. "We all work for him. Chemists, physicists, mathematicians, assistants, and right now, one of our main jobs is to perfect the incandescent lamp."

Bess pulled her face from the glass of the shack and looked at Francis. "You keep saying that, but what is an in-can-sent lamp?"

Hazel whispered in her ear. "I think he's talking about the light bulb," she said. "Mr. Edison's most famous invention."

"A light bulb? All this for a light bulb?" Bess yelled. Francis laughed.

Bess was right. There was a lot going on. And all to make one little light bulb.

Francis went on. "We work all day

and a lot of the night too. Mostly we've had failures. But today... it was all worth it." Francis gestured for the girls to follow him along the path. "Come on. Let's go inside, and I'll show you."

They walked onto the porch of the large white house. Francis stopped just before he opened the door. "This may seem like a lot of work for just a light bulb, but it's actually a lot more than that. It's about figuring out electricity, and ways to use it safely in your house. Pretty soon, people will be able to just flip a switch and have a light come on. Can you imagine it?"

Bess smirked. "Uh yeah..."

"And a practical light bulb that's cheap to produce, lasts a long time, and won't be too bright for inside the house is the first step," he said, opening the door.

The smell of machine parts and chemicals poured out from the house when the door opened. Hazel blinked to allow her eyes to adjust before stepping inside. Looking around, she couldn't believe it. She'd never seen anything like it before.

Chapter Eleven

Hazel and Bess followed Francis through the door and into the white building.

"So this is what an invention factory looks like," Hazel said, under her breath. "It's a house you can't live in."

She expected to see a living room with couches and a coffee table. But instead, the room was lined with long tables. Various machine parts and gadgets sat on all the different tables and cabinets. Men rushed about here and there.

Francis pointed around the room. "Most of the machines you see on this floor are Mr. Edison's famous inventions. They're just for display now, like over there. That's the famous phonograph, and of course, there's the electric pen and press."

Bess scrunched her face. So did Hazel. They had no idea what those machines were, and the one Francis said was "an electric pen" just looked like a couple of jars strung together with a string. Hazel thought she saw a pen dangling off the side of it, but what made it electric? It didn't have a plug or anything.

"Of course it doesn't have a plug," Hazel said to herself, suddenly remembering houses didn't have outlets yet.

"What are in those jars?" Bess asked, and for once, Hazel was glad to have a curious sister because she wanted to know too.

"Those jars are the battery for the pen," Francis said, moving on.

Hazel's mouth dropped. When she thought of batteries, she pictured small little things that went in the back of toys. These were huge jars.

There were similar jars sitting on a table, and more on the shelves behind it.

Francis seemed to sense the girls' curiosity. His eyebrows narrowed into angry darts like their grandfather's always did. "But remember. Don't touch anything."

He motioned for the girls to follow him up the stairs. Those angry eyebrows reminded Hazel of her grandfather and she wondered if maybe now was a good time to ask Francis about the other unexpected guest.

"So, Francis," she began as they reached the stairs. "Tell me more about the other strange guest you had today. Maybe we do know him, after all. I think you said his name was Burt. What was he like? Where was he from, did he say?"

"I remember he had dark hair, a beard and a mustache, but I don't remember where he said he was from.

Sorry."

The stairs that led to the second floor of the long white building were even more rickety than the ones at the old farmhouse. They seemed to creak a lot as they walked, and Hazel was happy when they'd reached the next floor.

Francis looked around, "I think that man's still here. Why don't you ask him yourself?"

Hazel's face dropped. *Did Francis just say their grandfather was still here?*

Chapter Twelve

Hazel searched the upstairs for a man who could possibly be their grandfather, but the whole second floor seemed like one long room full of men who looked like him. Bushy beards must've been very popular back in the 1800s.

The longer walls of the room had shelves lining them with metal parts and various containers full of what were probably chemicals. Large tables took up most of the room, and just like downstairs, workers rushed this way and that, chattering excitedly to one another.

Hazel looked carefully at all of them, but no one looked exactly like her grandfather, or like they were from the future.

"Do you see Grandpa anywhere?" Hazel whispered to her sister.

"What are you talking about?" Bess asked. "Did he follow us here?"

"No. We're here at the same time Grandpa was when he first stole those filament things. He's here somewhere too. A younger him."

"Wow," Bess said, but Hazel could tell

she wasn't really listening. She was fiddling with something behind her back like she was trying to hide it in her skirt. What in the world was her sister doing? Hazel looked behind her sister's back. Bess was carrying a jar from one of the batteries!

Thank goodness Francis hadn't seemed to notice. He was busy talking about who the men upstairs were and the many different experiments that were going on.

"Where did you get that?" Hazel whispered through gritted teeth.

"Downstairs. I just wanted to see what a jar battery looked like up close. That's all. So how do you think this thing works?"

Hazel rolled her eyes even though she

was curious about it too. "I have no idea, but you need to put it back before you get in trouble."

"Where do I put it?" Bess asked, handing it to Hazel. "I don't want it anymore. It's just a jar, and I'm tired of carrying it. Here, take it."

"I don't want it either," Hazel said, handing it back to Bess.

The contents of the jar sloshed up the sides as Bess and Hazel passed it to each other, causing the girls to lose their grip on its surface. The jar slipped from their fingers and fell to the floor.

Crash! Bits and pieces of broken glass went everywhere, sending liquid shooting off in all directions. The room instantly went silent. Everyone turned toward the sound.

Hazel and Bess stood guilty in front of the mess. There was no denying they were involved.

Bess shrugged. "Did anyone else see a green monster with a big snotty nose drop this jar?"

"Stop saying that!" Hazel snapped under her breath. "You've got to start taking responsibility for the stuff you do."

"You mean the stuff you did," she said. "You're the one who wouldn't take the jar."

Francis looked over. His face fell faster than a jar full of chemicals. "You!" He pointed at the girls. "Didn't I warn you both not to touch anything? Now look what you've done."

Hazel's face grew red. Once again, she was getting blamed for something Bess had done. "We can help you clean it up," she said, shooting her sister a mean look. This was all her fault.

"Don't worry, girls. We've got this," a couple of men said as they rushed over with a broom and a rag. "No worries. Looks like this jar only had a little salt water in it…"

Out of the corner of her eye, Hazel thought she saw a man with big shaggy eyebrows, a beard, and jeans run by while most everyone else was paying attention to the glass breaking. He had something in his hand – the filaments from the trunk – and he was sneaking down the stairs.

Hazel wanted to run after him to see if it was their grandpa, but Mr. Edison was yelling to her and Bess to come over to where he was at in the back of the room.

Uh oh. Hazel hoped the famous inventor wasn't mad at them for breaking his jar. Why was Bess always getting her into trouble?

Chapter Thirteen

Hazel and Bess slowly made their way to
the back of the room where Mr. Edison
stood, surrounded by workers. To Hazel's
surprise, they didn't seem mad about the
jar at all. They were all smiling and
laughing, patting each other on the back
and talking about how long they thought
the light bulb would last.

"So what do you think of the light bulb?" Mr. Edison asked the girls, pointing toward a tall wooden stand he was in front of. "Pretty impressive stuff we have here in the past."

The men laughed more.

Bess pulled her lips to the side. "Where's the light bulb?"

Hazel was just as confused as her sister. Attached to the tall wooden stand was a large dimly lit glowing piece of glass, but it didn't look at all like any of the light bulbs she'd ever seen before. It was a clear glass ball that seemed more like a fancy Christmas ornament than anything else, and why was it attached to this extra large stand? A soft glow came from the tiny black wire inside the glass that Hazel guessed was similar to the wires their grandfather stole. The ones these people were calling filaments.

"Isn't it amazing?" Francis said, gesturing for the men around the stand to step aside so the girls could see better. He looked right at Bess. "Now, don't touch anything."

Bess shook her head. "Why does everyone always say that to me?"

"It's been burning for almost 40 hours now," Francis explained. "We've finally completed the most important step in having safe, reliable lights inside our houses."

"I won't say we've completed it," Mr. Edison said. "But we're well on our way."

One of the workers patted him on the

back. "It's a shame we didn't get results sooner, though, huh?"

"Results! Why I have gotten a lot of results! I know several thousand things that won't work," Mr. Edison said. Everyone laughed, but Hazel could tell the inventor was serious. Mr. Edison went on. "Failure is a wonderful tool that can guide you to success if you look at it right. Sometimes, the only way to know what will work is by figuring out what won't."

Francis nodded in agreement. "Sometimes, it took us two or three days just to attach one of those filaments, only to have it break in the process, and we'd have to start all over again. Sometimes the filament wasn't made properly so it would burn out right away, or there was air in the bulb. That's why it's on this long stand, so we can vacuum the air out. The presence of air makes the temperature too hot, and the filament will burn too quickly... We learned from all of our mistakes."

Hazel looked at the coiled wire glowing in the middle of the glass bulb. She thought about how quickly she'd thrown her friendship bracelet across the room and given up on it.

Bess examined the bulb closely. "So, that black wire is the flip-a-ment?"

"Yep. It's called a fil-a-ment," Francis said. "Electricity passes through the filament, and causes it to light up. It's burning at a low voltage now. That just means not a lot of electricity is passing through it."

"Can you make it brighter?" Bess asked.

Mr. Edison laughed. "It's about time we found that out, wouldn't you all agree? Let's turn up the current." Mr. Edison turned a dial on the back of the stand. The lamp grew brighter. The men applauded.

"More," Bess yelled. Hazel tried to shush her, but the men cheered her on and Mr. Edison seemed to be enjoying the moment.

He turned it up higher and higher until, suddenly, the lamp grew extremely bright and... Blip! It burned out.

Oh no! Not again! Had her sister just broken the first light bulb on the day that was supposed to go down in history?

Chapter Fourteen

Bess shrugged. "Too bad that green monster told you to do that," she said, her face growing red with embarrassment. "I mean, I'm actually really sorry, Mr. Edison." Bess added, and Hazel could tell she meant it.

Mr. Edison laughed. "Don't be. We now know it can't handle that kind of voltage. We learn from our mistakes here, and that will be an area we'll plan to work on."

All the men applauded as Francis took the bulb off the stand.

"I'll take this down to be examined," he said leaving.

Mr. Edison yelled over the men's applause. "Mark the calendar, boys. This day will go down in history: October 21, 1879. Congratulations to us all."

"But it was just another failure," Hazel said.

"No, my dear girl, it was a success. Just because something doesn't do what you planned it to do doesn't mean it's useless," Mr. Edison said then added, "And I'll let you in on another little secret about life too. Many of life's failures are people who had no idea how close they were to success when they gave up." He smiled then walked away with the rest of the men.

Hazel reached in her pocket and pulled out the yellow, orange, and purple knotted lumpy friendship bracelet that Bess had given her before they left, and put it on. "Okay, Bess. Let's get going. I have a friendship bracelet I want to finish for you. And I'd like to get it done before dinner."

"I thought you gave up on that," Bess replied.

"Nope. I've decided to keep trying."

After thanking Mr. Edison and Francis, the girls left to find the time machine so they could go home. An afternoon breeze had picked up around

Menlo Park as they walked out of the long white house toward the bushes where the time machine was hidden, and Hazel rubbed her hands along her arms to warm herself up. The bracelet scratched her skin.

Hazel looked down at the bracelet. It was actually very beautiful in its own way, and Hazel felt terrible that she'd originally thought it was ugly just because it didn't look exactly like the picture in their book. She gave Bess a hug.

"What was that for?" Bess asked.

"Oh, just because a green monster with a big snotty nose told me to do it."

"You need to take more responsibility for the stuff you do," Bess said then laughed so hard she stumbled over a rock.

As they approached the spot where

they left the time machine, or where they thought they'd left it, they could tell right away that something was wrong. Even though they knew they should be able to see the plastic dome of the time machine's lid sticking out over the tops of the bushes, they only saw bushes.

Without saying a word, they both ran over and began searching through the scratchy branches of the thick hedge, peeking in at different spots, but nothing was there. The time machine was gone, and so was Froggenstein!

Chapter Fifteen

"What are we going to do?" Bess asked.

"It's okay." Hazel said, even though she was pretty sure it wasn't okay. She wanted to panic, but she knew she had to be calm. "We'll figure it out. It has to be here somewhere. We just need to look for it."

"How did it move?" Bess asked.

Hazel didn't have an answer.

The girls walked along the edge of the large fenced-in yard, around the side of the long, white house, and toward the building that Francis said was the machine shop. They saw one of the men from before, the one with the shaggy beard named Charles, about to enter the machine shop. The girls ran up to him. He stopped when he saw them approaching.

"Hello..." he said.

"Hello, Charles," Hazel began.

Bess interrupted her. "We're looking for a frog or a large..."

"Machine," Hazel said before her sister could blurt out what kind of a machine they were looking for.

"A frog?" Charles said. "So you're the owner of the frog. About 20 minutes ago, a man asked me to hold onto this little guy. I'm glad I didn't have to hold onto him for long."

The man went into the shop and brought out Froggenstein, still in his plastic cage.

Rrrrrrr-iiiibbbet

Bess's face lit up. She hugged the man and grabbed her frog.

Hazel was glad her sister had Froggenstein back, mostly because she knew Bess wasn't going to leave without him, and it was time to go. But where was the time machine?

"Did the man say anything else?"

Charles reached into his pocket and

pulled out a piece of paper. "As a matter of fact, he left you a note."

A note?

The girls thanked Charles and took the note. *Why on earth did someone leave them a note?*

Charles went back into the machine shop, and Hazel and Bess sat on a bench in front of the little house. Hazel opened the paper and read the note out loud.

"To the owner of the frog. I'm not sure who you are, but I know you're using a time machine that I designed. This note is to inform you that I've taken my machine back. Consider yourselves stuck in 1879."

Hazel couldn't believe their grandfather would write such a note or do such a thing. She knew he was mean, but she never thought he could be this mean. And what did he mean the time machine that he designed? The article Hazel found in the attic said a professor had designed the time machine. Their grandfather was just the thief who stole it.

Bess began to cry. "Who wrote that note?"

"Grandpa did. It's signed Burt Williamson. It was him."

"But why?"

"I don't know," she said, putting her arm around her sister. She didn't have an answer for that one.

"What are we going to do?" Bess said, stroking the saggy wet skin of her frog. "How could he do this to his own granddaughters?"

Hazel crumpled the note up and stuffed it in her pocket. "He didn't know we were his granddaughters when he did this. He just recognized his time machine when he saw it in the bushes, and thought someone had stolen it."

Bess's tears looked huge behind her thick glasses. "We're never going to get home."

"Well, we definitely won't if we give up." Hazel was surprised by what she was saying. "One thing's for sure. Grandpa couldn't have left in two time machines. He took ours, but his is still here someplace. All we have to do is find it!"

Bess got up and wiped her tears with the sleeve of her fancy ballet outfit. She suddenly seemed more determined than ever. "You're right," she said. "Let's find it."

"Maybe Charles has seen it," Hazel said, knocking on the machine shop door. Charles opened it.

"Just one last thing," Hazel said to the man. "Have you seen any strange machines around here..."

"We have many strange machines around here. This is Thomas Edison's invention factory, after all. You'll have to be more specific," he said.

"A new machine. One you've never seen before. It had a large dome with a round lid and a chair inside..." Hazel began.

"You know, a time machine," Bess said. "It was a time machine that takes you to the past or the future."

Hazel shot her sister a look. *Why did*

her sister always say the wrong things?

Charles laughed. "That's right," he said, winking at Hazel. "I'd forgotten you're both from the future. Well, I haven't seen your time machine, ladies…"

Charles's wink reminded Hazel of that morning in the living room when her grandfather had winked at them. He'd also mumbled something under his breath at that time too. Hazel thought he was just being crazy, but then, maybe he was giving them information. Maybe he was helping them. *What had he said?*

"Behind the glassblower's shop!" Hazel blurted out without worrying what Charles would think of her or the time machine. "The time machine is behind the glassblower's shop! Remember what

Grandpa said this morning?" Hazel was jumping up and down now. It had all made sense. "Those filaments weren't left in the trunk by mistake. Grandpa knows everything, and he's begun helping us!"

Hazel wasn't sure she was right, but she and Bess took off running toward the glassblower's shop to see, leaving Charles standing at the door, scratching his head.

Chapter Sixteen

Outside the small building that the girls knew as the glassblower's shop, Hazel and Bess saw the time machine right away, peeking out from the bushes that surrounded the area.

Bess hugged Hazel. "I'm so happy you're finally right about something!"

Hazel shot her sister a look as she

opened the dome lid of the machine. "It looks exactly the same!" Hazel said, getting in. "Come on. Let's go home. I'm hungry and homemade anything sounds good right now."

Bess sat down next to her sister and the girls strapped themselves in. "Wait a second," Bess said. "Where's the secret compartment? It's supposed to be right here." She pointed to the empty place under the control panel.

Oh no! Hazel thought to herself. This machine wasn't exactly the same at all. It was missing the most important part. The secret compartment, which was the only way they knew how to start the machine up. Maybe they really were trapped in 1879.

A tear ran down Hazel's face, and she quickly wiped it away before Bess could see. A part of her wanted to give up and walk away crying, but she knew she had to be strong for her sister. Besides, if she gave up now, she might not ever know just how close they were to succeeding, and she hoped they were pretty close.

"We've got to think of something," she said.

Bess shrugged and pushed buttons. "Okay, let's figure this out..."

Hazel rolled her eyes. While Bess played, Hazel opened the note from their grandfather again. Maybe, somehow, there was a clue there.

He must've been in an angry hurry when he wrote it. It was scribbled on the back of a torn-in-half flyer. Hazel pulled out the bookmark she found before they left. She held them together. They were a perfect match, only one half was yellowed and old, and the other was new.

She could finally read the whole flyer!

It's science fiction in real life.

Professor Burt Williamson will demonstrate an actual time machine on...

Professor Burt Williamson? So, their grandfather hadn't stolen the time machine from a professor after all. He was the professor! This was all so strange. Hazel had always thought her grandparents were farmers...

The glassblower's shop door swung open and out walked a little man with a large mustache. He was carrying a metal stick with a glowing red wad of goop stuck to the end of it. Hazel guessed he must've been in the process of making some sort of glass.

"Hey!" yelled the man, waving his arms around, motioning to Hazel and Bess from his door.

"Hi," Bess replied, waving back, with a big warm smile.

"I don't think he's being friendly," Hazel said, noticing the man's face was almost as red as the goop he was carrying.

"What are you doing? Kids can't play here. That machine is one of Mr. Edison's inventions. Go away before you break it!"

Hazel knew he must've thought this machine belonged to Mr. Edison, but he was wrong. It didn't. There was probably no way to convince him of that, though. She needed to figure this whole thing out, and fast.

Bess pushed more and more combinations of buttons as the man walked toward them with the red-hot glass.

"Maybe pushing red, blue and yellow together will work..." she said, pushing buttons.

The angry glassblower was still yelling as he walked closer to the girls, but his accent was so thick Hazel could hardly make out what he was saying. "Get out! You have no business here. Get out!"

Hazel's heart raced as the man approached. What were they going to do?

"Come on, Bess. We'd better r-r-un." Hazel said, stuffing the flyer into her pocket. One of the halves dropped under the control panel just as Bess pushed some buttons. A large, powerful rumble came up from under the machine. First slow then faster.

It had started! It had started!

Hazel quickly buckled them in as the glassblower's mouth fell open in disbelief. He dropped his hot stick, which landed right on his foot. He jumped back and grabbed his foot.

Hazel tried to stop herself from laughing when she saw him hopping in pain.

The glassblower suddenly got angrier. He ran for the time machine and reached out for the girls.

"Hurry, Bess! Push more buttons!"

Hazel said, confident her sister would figure it out.

The man reached the machine and pulled on Hazel's arm. She screamed just as Bess pushed another button...

Blip.

They were gone.

Chapter Seventeen

Hazel blinked her eyes into focusing. The
room they were in was dark, just like their
grandparents' attic, but different. She
looked around. From what she could tell,
the girls were in an attic, all right, but not
the farmhouse one. This place was small
and cramped full of dolls, notebooks, and

old machine parts strewn all over the place.

Bess was by the door. She shushed Hazel when she saw her.

"What's going on?" Hazel asked.

Bess shrugged. "We're not in our attic."

Hazel rolled her eyes. She already knew that part.

"But I think I hear Grandpa," Bess said. "And some kid."

Hazel put her ear by the door and listened too.

A familiar voice came from downstairs. It was definitely their grandfather. Hazel knew they must've followed him here from Thomas Edison's place somehow, wherever here was. But who was the kid?

"So I get to come tomorrow, right?" the little girl asked in a squeaky voice that seemed oddly familiar.

"Of course," their grandfather replied.

The little girl squealed. "We're going to be rich and famous! I can't wait to see my friends' faces when they see your time machine! It really works, right?"

"Yes, Kay. It really works."

"Really? Because nobody believes you. They think you're..." the little girl hesitated.

"I know everyone thinks I'm crazy. But don't you worry. We'll show 'em. I just got back from another trip. I have lots of proof."

Hazel whispered to Bess, "Oh my

goodness! I think that little girl is Mom!"

RRRRRRR---ibbbbbet!

"Shhh," Bess said to her frog, but it was too late, not that a frog would listen to shushing anyway. The voices downstairs stopped.

Hazel heard footsteps coming up the stairs and she looked around for a place to hide. She noticed a very large blanket, off in a dark corner, that looked like it was hiding something familiar.

"Come on," she said, yanking her sister by the arm and pulling her over to the blanket. Hazel's friendship bracelet flew off her wrist and across the room.

"Hey! Why are you yanking me?" Bess asked.

"I see the other time machine. The

one Grandpa took earlier. Let's go. Hurry!"

"But your bracelet," Bess said, trying to yank free from Hazel's grasp.

"We don't have time," Hazel whisper-yelled. "We'll make more, I promise."

"I don't want to make another one. That one was perfect."

"Who's up there?" their grandfather called out as he approached the attic door. His footsteps got louder and quicker, and the girls could tell he was almost there.

Hazel knew they were going to be in big trouble if they got caught. Their grandfather wouldn't know they were his grandkids at this point in time, and there was no telling what he would do if he caught two kids snooping around his time machine.

Hazel yanked the blanket off the other time machine, and Bess reluctantly got inside, sticking Froggenstein in his compartment and pushing the green button.

Their grandfather opened the attic door just as the rumbling started on the time machine's engine. He turned his head to say something, and Hazel couldn't help but notice how different he looked. His eyebrows and beard were still bushy, but they weren't gray yet. He didn't have the shriveled, wrinkled face of an old man. His skin was smooth and full of life. His eyes widened as he watched the girls at the time machine.

"Good-bye, Grandpa," Bess yelled over the sound of the rumbling. "Try to find my friendship bracelet, okay? It's somewhere in your attic, and we want it back!"

To Hazel's surprise, their grandpa didn't seem angry anymore. He even kind of halfway waved to them as they disappeared from his sight.

Blip.

Chapter Eighteen

It felt good to be back in the farmhouse living room, eating homemade biscuits, and working on another friendship bracelet with Bess, even though neither one of them was getting it right.

Hazel's fingers tangled in the thread again, and she smiled as she yanked them out.

She could hardly believe everything that had happened that day. Their grandfather definitely knew they were using his time machine – and he didn't seem to mind. In fact, he was helping them.

Hazel wanted to talk to him about the time machine, but how? They didn't really know their grandfather and he seemed so mean.

Hazel had more questions than answers. She pulled out the flyer from her back pocket. Too bad it wasn't the whole flyer, and most of it was so faded, it was unreadable.

Come see a demonstration of the world's first time machine at the fair this Saturday! Local professor has proof...

Hazel shook her head. Something

must've happened that day, the day of the fair and the time machine demonstration, but what? What was the big family secret?

Something soft smacked Hazel across the face. She looked down. A wadded mass of friendship bracelet was on her lap, and her sister was laughing.

"I made you another one," Bess said.

Hazel put the paper back in her pocket and tugged her hand through the bracelet lump. "Thanks," she said. She and Bess were having more fun than ever.

Bess sat down next to Hazel and pointed to the page in the book with the turquoise and black friendship bracelet.

"Can we really make something that looks like that?" she asked.

"Maybe not the first time we try it.

But we can keep trying until we get it right."

"Ok," Bess smiled. "Because I want to make it for Grandpa."

The door opened and their mother walked in followed by their grandparents. Their mother looked shocked. "Wow. Have you girls been working on those friendship bracelets all day? How many have you done?"

Hazel shrugged. "Well, I haven't been able to get any of them right yet. But I've figured out 1,000 ways not to make a friendship bracelet, so that's something."

Bess and Hazel laughed. Their mother gave them a strange look and kissed them both on the head.

Pointing to the turquoise bracelet in

the book, Bess said, "We're going to make this one next... for Grandpa."

Their mother smiled. "That's so sweet. Isn't it, Dad?" She walked into the kitchen. "Then you can finally get rid of that old faded one you've been lugging around for years."

Both of the girls looked at their grandfather for a reaction, but he didn't seem to care that they were making him a bracelet. He only grunted and followed their mother into the kitchen with their grandmother. Maybe he was just as mean as they thought. How were they ever going to talk to him about anything, much less something as important as the time machine?

A few minutes later, he came back in

and laid something on the coffee table in front of Bess and Hazel. It was an old faded lumpy yellow, orange, and purple friendship bracelet with an orange bead tied to it.

"A long time ago, a mysterious little girl in my attic asked me to find her bracelet and give it back to her," he said. "I think I can finally make good on that promise."

Hazel couldn't believe it. That had just happened. The girls hugged their grandfather tightly around the neck for what seemed like minutes. Maybe it wasn't going to be so hard to talk to him after all.

"And now," he whispered, his mouth barely moving through his thick beard. "I'm going to need both of your help…"

--The End –

Hi. Thank you so much for reading my book. I hope you liked reading it as much as I liked writing it. And if you did, please consider telling your friends about it and writing a review. Having reviews is really important to authors. They help us spread the word about our books. Plus, I'd love to know what you think!

Here are the other books in the Time Machine Girls series if you're interested:

Book One: Secrets
Book Two: Never Give Up
Book Three: Courage
Book Four: Teamwork

And if you'd like to know when new books are coming out, just have your parents sign up for my newsletter list on my website www.ernestinetitojones.com.

Read on for more about Thomas Edison.

Thanks again!
Ernestine

More About Thomas Edison
(or what I learned when I researched this book)

Growing up, I was always taught that Thomas Edison invented the light bulb. Later on, I found out it's a little more complicated than that.

Although a "light bulb" had already been invented at the time, it was expensive to run, burnt out quickly, was dangerous, and electricity wasn't even in homes yet.

A lot had to be studied and learned about electrical currents and practical lighting before anything could happen, and many inventors were interested in the project. Thomas Edison was one of them. Because he was a well-known inventor at the time with many successful inventions in electricity, it wasn't hard for him to find rich investors to loan him money toward this project. That means they didn't "give" Edison the money. They expected a "return on investment" (called an R.O.I. in the business world), which is just a fancy way of saying they expected to make their money back and then some. In this case, they expected to make money on not only a light bulb design, but they also expected to charge people every month for electricity.

It was the beginning of a huge industry, and Edison was under a lot of pressure to figure things out. He built Menlo Park as a laboratory for his inventions, and he hired many people to help him – mathematicians, physicists, a glass blower, a machinist, various assistants, and other helpers too. It was the world's first research and development laboratory. Menlo Park grew into a small village that still exists today, but not in New Jersey anymore. Most of the structures were preserved and moved from New Jersey to Greenfield Village in Dearborn, Michigan by Henry Ford in 1929. You can visit it there if you want.

We have lights and electricity in our houses thanks in large part to the experiments done not just by Thomas Edison in Menlo

Park but also by many other inventors like him around the world who also worked in the electrical industry at the time – building and learning from each other's successes... and failures.

It's actually really interesting stuff, so if you want to know more – I don't blame you. I did too when I was researching this book.

Parts of the Story That Are Real:
The two assistants described in this story are Francis Jehl (the man with the mustache) and Charles Batchelor (the one with the beard) were actual assistants of Thomas Edison, even though the story of Hazel and Bess is fiction. Much of what is described in *The Time Machine Girls* about Menlo Park and all the people who worked there came from a book written by Francis Jehl called *Menlo Park Reminiscences: Volume One.*

Thomas Edison was 32 at the time this story takes place, and many of the quotes he says in this story are ones he supposedly said in real life including the ones about failure. He was a very witty inventor! And he really did say he failed that many times before he got the light bulb right, so never give up. Failing is an amazing learning tool you can use to get to success.

The incandescent lamp (light bulb) was declared a success on October 21, 1879. And according to Francis's book, the light bulb lasted for 40 hours until Edison turned up the voltage and it burned out. Of course, he wasn't really coaxed to do it by a little girl in a superhero costume.

What I hope you got from this book – never give up. When you fail, it doesn't mean you're a failure. It means you're learning how to succeed. We can learn a lot from our mistakes if we look at them the right way, and never give up trying.

Anyway, I hope you enjoyed the book. I learned a lot from researching it, and it was a lot of fun to write.

Made in the USA
Middletown, DE
30 June 2022